BON ODORI DANCER

KAREN KAWAMOTO MCCOY

Illustrations by
CAROLINA YAO

POLYCHROME PUBLISHING CORPORATION
Chicago, Illinois

Library of Congress

Cataloging-in-Publication Data

McCoy, Karen Kawamoto.
Bon Odori Dancer / Written by Karen Kawamoto McCoy;
Illustrations by Carolina Yao
        p.   cm.

Summary: Keiko is the clumsiest girl in her Japanese dance
class, but when the other girls stop laughing at her and start
helping her, they all perform well at the Obon festival.

ISBN No. 1-879965-16-X: $14.95
[1. Dance— Fiction.   2. Japanese Americans — Fiction.]

I. Yao, Carolina, ill.
II. Title.

PZ7.M47841447Bo 1998
[E]—dc21

        98-12050
          CIP
            AC

This is a new book, written and illustrated especially for
Polychrome Books
First Edition, Fall, 1999

Designed, produced and published by
Polychrome Publishing Corporation
4509 North Francisco Avenue
Chicago, Illinois 60625-3808
(773) 478-4455 Fax: (773) 478-0786
website: http://home.earthlink.net/~polypub/

Editorial Director, Sandra S. Yamate
Production Coordinator, Brian M. Witkowski

Printed in Hong Kong
By O.G. Printing Productions Ltd.
10 9 8 7 6 5 4 3 2 1

ISBN 1-879965-16-X

"To my grandparents, Ichiro and Ito Kawamoto."
KAREN KAWAMOTO MCCOY

"To my mom, for her love and tremendous support and always believing in me."
CAROLINA YAO

Left, right, THUD! Keiko crashed on the hard floor.

Eleven giggling girls, in t-shirts and shorts, twirled around her. CLICK, CLACK echoed the kachi-kachi sticks in their hands. Their bodies swirled in the opposite direction. PLINK, PLINK ended the soft shamisen music. One by one, the dancers bowed to their teacher, Mrs. Hinatsu.

Embarrassed, Keiko crawled to where the others were kneeling. Obon odori, or the Obon festival, when they would perform this traditional dance, was only two weeks away. For the millionth time, she wished her feet would go in the proper directions: Not left foot, right and right foot, left!

"You're just not trying hard enough," complained Amy. Amy was the most graceful dancer in their group.

"I do try!" exclaimed Keiko. The problem was her crazy feet. They never wanted to follow the other dancers.

Mrs. Hinatsu clapped her hands for attention. "That was better. You're all showing improvement."

Amy's mouth dropped in surprise. "All of us?"

Mrs. Hinatsu nodded.

Eleven pairs of eyes focused on Keiko. A giant lump formed in her throat. Why, oh why, had she ever wanted to take this class? It was such a long time since she had seen the dancers perform at last year's Obon festival. How she had longed to be a part of it! What a beautiful way to honor their ancestors she had thought.

Mrs. Hinatsu clapped her hands again. "Everyone back on the floor! There's only a short time left to practice."

Keiko concentrated hard on her feet. Left, right, swirl! Click, clack with the kachi-kachi sticks. Right, left, twirl! Oops! Her sticks clattered to the floor. She stooped to pick them up. Swirl, swirl, bang! Crash! Amy and Mariko collided with her. Now three girls sat heaped on the floor.

Stopping the music, Mrs. Hinatsu shook her head.

Amy rolled her eyes. "Why don't you pay attention?"

Keiko's cheeks turned the color of cherries. She clutched the sticks in her hands and took her place in the circle of girls. This time, she was determined not to drop the sticks or do the wrong step.

Left, right, swirl! Click, clack with the sticks. Oops, a little too close to Mariko! Keiko scooted to her left and twirled several times. The soft music faded and giggles filled

the air. Looking up, Keiko gasped in horror. The rest of the class was on the other side of the room!

"Quiet, please!" exclaimed Mrs. Hinatsu, but even she looked flustered. "Let's start fresh next time," she said in a tired voice. "Class is dismissed."

Tears swelled in Keiko's eyes. "I quit! I'll never learn the routine!" she moaned.

"Nonsense," said Mariko, putting an arm around her. "You only need more practice."

"Or two new feet," murmured Amy.

Mariko frowned. "Some people take a little longer."

"We could hold extra practice sessions," suggested one of the girls.

"Yes, let's!" exclaimed another.

Sadly, Keiko shook her head. "Thanks for trying to help, but it's no use."

"Yes, it is," replied the girls. "Just try."

The next two weeks were grueling. Keiko practiced twice each day, during dance class in the morning, and afterwards at Mariko's house. She still made mistakes. Sticks clattered to the floor. Stumbles and bumps occurred. Heels were scraped and toes were squashed, but this time, no laughter filled the room.

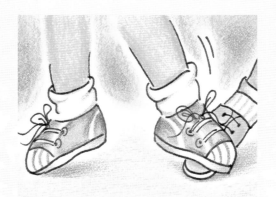

Instead, the girls took turns, coaching and encouraging Keiko. Slowly the steps became easier. Left, right, swirl! Click, clack with the sticks! Right, left, twirl! Only Amy was skeptical.

"There's still Obon," she reminded them, rubbing her shin, where Keiko had accidentally kicked her.

The night of the Obon festival arrived. Keiko and her friends gathered early at Ichiban Park. Each girl wore a yellow obi around her red kimono and rainbow colored ribbons in her hair. Six shamisen players and a drummer were starting to play. Throngs of people began to fill the park.

Keiko felt her knees wobble. She wasn't ready to dance. She needed more practice. She glanced at her innocent-looking feet. What were *they* going to do tonight? Panicking, she turned to slip away. Ooof! She bumped into Amy!

"Where are you going? We're next."

"I can't do it," Keiko cried. "You were right! I know I'll do something wrong."

"Hmpf! You can't give up now!" replied Amy. "The others are counting on you."

"But I'm scared," gasped Keiko. "I can't do it."

"Just *try!*"

"But what if I make a mistake? How will it look if I mix up the steps?"

Amy looked at her. "How will *they* feel if you don't even try?" She gestured toward the other girls standing near the edge of the stage. "How will *you* feel?"

Keiko was startled. She stared at the eager faces of her friends as they waited for their turn to perform. She thought about Mariko and the other girls and all their extra practice, just to help her. She remembered the words of encouragement they'd offered, no matter how clumsy she'd been. How could she let them down? Swallowing hard, Keiko followed Amy toward the stage. Ready or not, she must dance!

Mrs. Hinatsu signaled to the musicians. PLINK, PLINK sang the shamisen. BOOM BOOM rang the drum. THUMPITY–THUMP went Keiko's heart. It was time!

Keiko took a deep breath and forced her trembling legs to move. Left, right, swirl. She danced dangerously close to Mariko.

"Relax," whispered Mariko.

Keiko held her breath and struck her

kachi-kachi sticks. CLICK, CLACK! Then she stepped to the right and almost stumbled.

"It's okay," whispered another girl.

Nervously, Keiko continued. Left, right, swirl. Right, left, twirl. CLICK–PLOP! One of her sticks banged on the ground. Panic flooded through her. Should she pick it up? Could she reach it? A sharp nudge saved her.

"Use mine!" Amy thrust one of her sticks into Keiko's hands.

Trembling, Keiko clutched the sticks. Left, right, swirl. Right, left twirl. Finally the drum thumped its last beat. BOOM, BOOM! The shamisen sang their final notes. PLINK, PLINK!

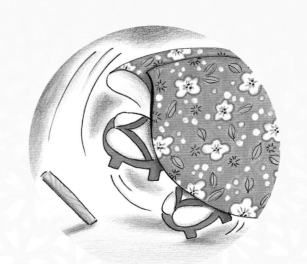

It was over! Mrs. Hinatsu was smiling.
The girls linked arms and bowed to the
clapping crowd. Someone snapped their
picture. Then, "We did it! We did it!" Mariko
and the other girls were jumping up and
down. Keiko smiled with relief.

Slowly Keiko followed Mariko and the
other girls toward the north end of the park
where there were snow cones for all the
children.

Someone poked Keiko in the back.
Whirling around, she came face to face
with Amy.

"Good job," Amy said. Then she smiled.

Keiko felt like singing . . . or dancing! Tonight, she had tried her hardest. She wasn't perfect, but she had tried and even Amy knew it. She was glad she had done it. It felt good.

Grinning, Keiko skipped alongside Amy, Mariko and the other girls. Eating their snow cones, they laughed and chattered, as they made plans for next year's Obon odori.

OBON is an abbreviation of *urabon*, the Japanese transliteration of the Sanskrit word *Ullambana* that literally means, "to hang upside down." This word implies the suffering one has to bear, whether spiritual or physical, when being upside down.

Although the word "bon" itself comes from the Buddhist word *urabon*, Bon was not originally a Buddhist observance. For the most part Obon is of purely Japanese origin and it's generally thought that Buddhism may have become linked accidentally.

The actual customs tend to vary from area to area, from different foods eaten to different clothing worn, but the idea that for a few days the living and the dead are reunited for a friendly get-together should always be constant.

Obon is a very special time. It allows us to strengthen our connection to our family ancestors. Without their life we could not have been born as a precious human being. It is both a time of reflection and celebration, and an acknowledgment of both past and present.

The Bon dance is a dance for the harmony of people where everyone moves their arms in graceful gestures and steps one after the other.

The Obon festival, an ancient festival, is among the world's most colorful religious and cultural observances. After New Year's Day it is probably the most important date on the Japanese calendar. The festival of Obon is the Buddhist All Soul's Day. In Japan it is generally celebrated in mid-August, but in the United States it may be observed in July or August.

While the Buddhist principle of Universal Harmony seems unrealistic in our fragmented and divided society and world, it is an ideal which challenges us and to which we should aspire.

TANKO BUSHI (COAL MINER'S DANCE)

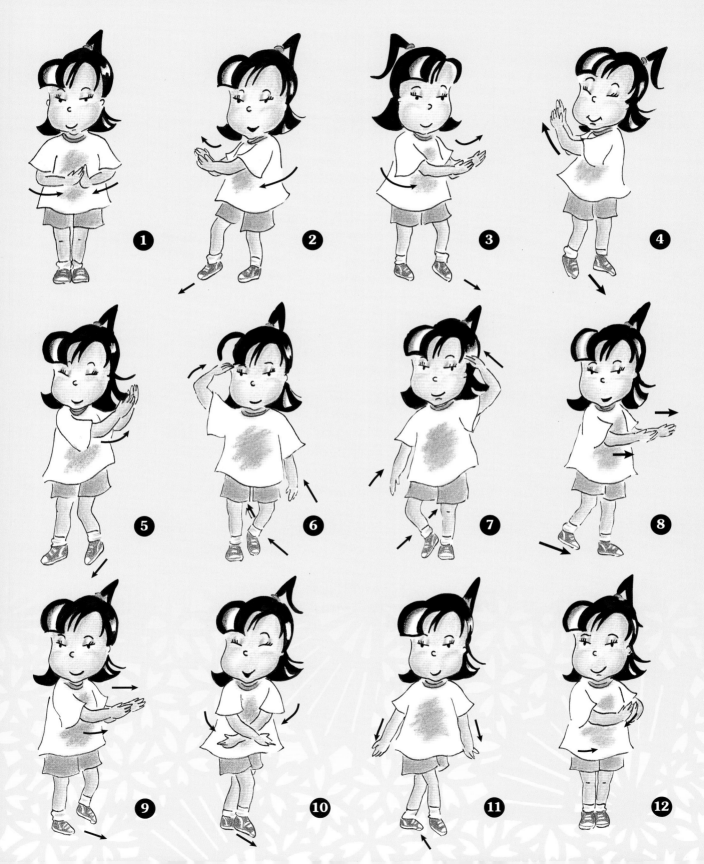

Acknowledgements

Polychrome Publishing appreciates the support, help and encouragement received from Lia Lauryn Chan; Tiana Chan; Theodora B. Chann; Hon. Hannah Chow; Elyse Cerney; Mary L. Doi; Jean M. Fujiu; Sharon Harada; Michael and Kay Janis; the Japanese American Service Committee; Leonard Joy and Suzanne Sawada and Stephen, Nicole, and Christie; Kay Kawaguchi; Yvonne Lau; Mitchell and Laura Witkowski; George and Vicki Yamate; and Kiyo Yoshimura. Without them, this book would not have been possible.

About Polychrome Publishing

Founded in 1990, Polychrome Publishing Corporation is an independent press located in Chicago, Illinois, producing children's books for a multicultural market. Polychrome books introduce characters and illustrate situations with which children of all colors can readily identify. They are designed to promote racial, ethnic, cultural and religious tolerance and understanding. We live in a multicultural world. We at Polychrome Publishing believe that our children need a balanced multicutural education if they are to thrive in that world. Polychrome Books can help create that balance.